Monkey Tales

SALLY JO MARTINE

COVER: Nadine (Pages 18 - 19); Photo: Alan Francescutti

ISBN-13: 978-0615756554
ISBN-10: 0615756557

DEDICATION

Dedicated to my mother, Helen Martin, whose playful spirit
flourished along "the monkey trail" and whose inspired delight
gave birth to "Monkey Tales."

AUTHOR'S NOTE

These handmade, one-of-a-kind original monkeys discovered themselves somewhere between the assemblage of their body parts and subsequent adornment.

Each monkey has their own story, yet they share a common purpose – to bring levity, light, and joy into the lives of others.

VISIT US ONLINE

OneBeingHuman-sjm.com

ACKNOWLEDGMENTS

Many have kindly contributed their time, expertise, and playful enthusiasm to my sock monkey adventures. I'm grateful to each of them: Zipprea Arbuckle for her wide-open heart and a friendship spanning more than three decades; Larry Balentine for his powerful and penetrating vision – and for having my back; Shirli Barovich for believing in the monkeys and believing in me every step of the way; Clinton Bech for fanning the monkey flames at family gatherings; Dominique Cantwell and the entire BPA staff for graciously hosting *The Full Monkey* and for their kind support of my monkey journey; Lee Cobert and Diane Ryon for nourishing my creative spirit; Don Flora for his gentle ways, expertise, and kind assistance with design; Alan Francescutti – photographer extraordinaire – for his extreme patience, keen eye, and reliable wit; Beverly Gilyeart for giving Samba and Rufus a loving home; the administrative, nursing, kitchen, and maintenance staff at Liberty Shores for their excellent care of my mother during her twilight years; my mother, Helen Martin who proudly hosted countless monkey sleep-overs, and who never failed to inquire about "the next" monkey; Ed Parker for generous design and printing of The Full Monkey calendar (prototype); Rex-zane Rudee (Hudson Photography) for photographs and training; Mark Sell for innovative and resourceful design of the monkey stands; David and Jodi Richardson for tirelessly promoting the monkeys with family and friends (and for David's well-honed editing skills); Val Richardson for her sharp wit and wisdom; the Washington C.A.S.H. program for empowering entrepreneurs with resources and inspiration to cultivate their success; and Christine Whitehall for her insightful feedback, creative genius, and genuine interest in meeting each new monkey and welcoming it to the tribe. All photographs are courtesy of Alan Francescutti, unless otherwise noted.

AGATHA

A simple woman with a wonderfully complex mind, Agatha is a bit old fashioned and finds herself frequently yearning for the "good old days." A monkey of many talents, she enjoys baking, canning, and sewing. She lives on a ranch, where she enjoys a quiet life with her dogs and looks forward to a nap every afternoon. Her family and friends admire her skill in the kitchen and are ever ready to taste her down-home cooking.

ALABASTER SNOWBALL

A tiny, dwarf-like creature from the North Country, Alabaster Snowball administers Santa's Naughty & Nice list. Youthful but immortal, his magical powers allow him to control what people see and experience. His Elfin history is strongly linked to Germanic paganism and he is often associated with the Amanita "magic" mushrooms familiar in art and psychedelic experiences.

ALEK

Locally known for his trademark abilities and innovative methods as a craftsman, Alek is broadly appreciated as a defender of humankind. He holds a deep inner desire for a stable, loving family and community, and he has a pressing need to work with others and share his expertise. Idealistic at heart, he gives back to his tight-knit Island community in consistently imaginative, innovative, and intuitive ways, mostly through his role as Technical Director for a flourishing theater company. Photo courtesy of Larry Balentine.

BAILEY

Bailey has spent his entire life back stage serving as prop master, costume designer, and set designer. Secretly, he yearns for an on-stage role, and he had desperately hoped to be cast in *The Full Monty*, which the local performing arts center staged just last year. He wasn't selected, but since the spring musical was so enthusiastically-received by his small community, Bailey is confident it will be reprised in an upcoming season.

BIKER DUDE

Biker Dude likes to think of himself as a tough guy from the 50s. He likens himself to "the Fonz" in his roughed up leathers, but he has a soft spot for Sarah, and he just can't get enough of her. He's seen the way Herman ogles her, but Biker Dude is totally secure in his manhood, and he knows that all he has to do is say "heyyy," snap his fingers, and Sarah will come running.

HARVEY

"Now you see him, now you don't!" Harvey is a benevolent but mischievous nature-spirit bunny monkey. He's been known to stop space and time, has a special talent as a shape-shifter, is capable of human speech, and is especially fond of introverts. He often gives advice and leads people away from harm. An enthusiastic creature of Celtic folklore, Harvey likes to dance a jig in his spare time, frequently spicing it up with some tumbling and back layouts.

HERMAN

Bookish at heart, Herman is a studious loner. He's curious about Sarah, however, and he finds himself frequently fantasizing about her string of pearls and long striped legs. Though not a fighting monkey, Herman's seen the chauvinistic ways Biker Dude treats Sarah, and lately he's taken to aggressive posturing whenever Biker Dude's around.

ISIS

High priestess, chameleon, and a duplicitous shape-shifter, Isis is known for her seductive, and sometimes deceptive ways. She represents fecundity and the lunar flux of the female body. Trained in the highest magic, she often serves as the portal between humanity and divinity. Photo courtesy of Larry Balentine.

MARGE

Marge is free spirited and unconventional and longs to make her mark in the fashion industry. She's determined to have a hair style that others will want to emulate. She contributes her talents to the local theater, where she frequently volunteers.

NADINE

Dancing is the highest form of expression in Nadine's world. Previously lacking the courage to follow her own inner beat, she's ecstatic to have landed a role in *Hairspray*, and she's especially relieved that she hasn't had to resort to pole dancing. In fact, her life has taken an unexpectedly wholesome and hopeful turn since she encountered the older (but attractive!) Sven on a back-country ski outing.

OLAF

Growing up under the watchful eye of his grandfather Sven, Olaf learned the ways of the North Country at an early age. His athletic prowess revealed itself in youthful adventures ranging from dog sledding to luge, speed skating, and freestyle skiing. He's grateful for his genetic code and the familial vitality evidenced by Sven's energetic romantic pursuits.

21

PABLO

Happiest spending time in his studio creating, Pablo views the world as a collection of shapes and colors that mingle in mysterious and wondrous ways. His early escapades with Alabaster catalyzed and crystallized his depth of vision and left an indelible psychedelic mark on his body of work, which gained praise the world over from notoriously puritanical art critics.

PEARL

Pearl rarely goes unnoticed. Between her strangely penetrating gaze and her low slung, but old-fashioned bathing suit, she draws a crowd wherever she goes. She's a real bathing beauty, despite her susceptibility to sunburn.

PHINEAS

A legendary showman and circus promoter, Phineas is best remembered for founding the first modern three-ring circus. Despite his standard dress of "bronco chaps," his early rodeo adventures often go unmentioned. Phineas snuck in a quick "nip" before his turn at the photo shoot.

POLLY

An American madam of Russian-Jewish origin, Polly immigrated to the United States just before WWI. As a young woman, she became involved in the Manhattan theater community, where she roomed with an actress and showgirl. Polly opened her first bordello under mob protection in 1920 and became highly successful. One of her later establishments featured hidden stairways and secret doorways and was frequented by an array of legendary patrons.

RAFIYA

Practiced in the mystical shamanic arts, Rafiya fluently communes with the spirit realm, divining the true nature of all things. She longs to find a community in which her spirituality will flourish, where her practice will ignite the heart flames of all who surround her.

ROBERT(A)

Robert(a) loves the way women's clothes drape over his chest, he delights in the fluttering of false eyelashes on his cheeks, and he thrills at the attention he draws from both men and women. After decades of repression, he's entranced to finally be who he really is.

RUFUS

If he looks a little bit worried...it's because he is!
Perplexed by his master's mood swings and
dismayed by her periodic absences, Rufus feels
every emotional overtone and undertone and only
wishes he could make Samba feel happier.

SAMBA

An overnight dancing sensation, Samba has captured the hearts of the globe. Her graceful agility and youthful flexibility fueled a meteoric rise to the top, where her skills stand uncontested in the international dance scene. When not on stage or out of town, she enjoys taking Rufus on long runs through the Grand Forest.

SARAH

Despite her royal descent, Sarah's escapades make frequent headlines in the most scandalous tabloids. Secretly, she's smitten with Biker Dude, who fuels her fiercest "bad-boy" rock-n-roll fantasies. Recently, she's become so obsessive that she's even ignoring Scamp...much to her neighbors' dismay.

SCAMP

High pitched and demanding, Scamp's yips are persistent and tragically (for the neighbors) hard to ignore. He's overwhelmingly anxious to convey his adoration for his master at every opportunity, whether Sarah is coming, going, or effectively ignoring him - a condition that Scamp seems bound and determined to change.

41

SKYHAWK

A monkey shaman of distinctive powers, Skyhawk
dwells in a liminal sphere, spanning the threshold
of what is and what is yet to be. He serves as an
intermediary between the human and spirit
worlds and lends a restorative balance and
wholeness to whatever space he inhabits. He
often visits other worlds and dimensions to invoke
wellness and bring guidance to his community.

SVEN

Elderly now, Sven fondly recalls his boyhood days of cross-country skiing, when the Scandinavian countryside was all but silent, barring the steady, clicking rhythm of his skis. A newcomer to a small seaside village in the Pacific Northwest, Sven is determined to preserve his well-toned physique, and he frequently goes on outings with Alpine Adventures (a local singles group), through which he recently met a fetching young dancer. Nadine's youthful and athletic form makes him feel like a young man again.

YETI

Yeti works hard to keep the home fires burning and often treks for miles to gather wood that's just right. He's solid, steady, and reliable, but his Olympic Peninsula neighbors often go for weeks, or even months, without seeing him.

THE MONKEY STORY

"Oh, Sally..." she said, on opening it. For her 89th birthday, I had been sorely challenged to find anything...anything at all to breathe life into her spirit and make her days less long. But my mother's very first sock monkey surprised us both. Tears of delight blanketed her face. She stretched out her arms, reached for it, and simply stared. Her mouth curled gleefully into a little-girl smile, and with eyes glistening, she cooed again, "Oh, ohhhhh, Sally..."

Amazingly, the monkey conveyed my mother straight to her youth, offering a direct portal into carefree days, where "hope" colored her entire horizon.

"Miss Princess Annabelle Liberty Shores," aka "Gertrude," became my mother's new best friend. Mom proudly carted her along everywhere, and promptly enlisted the nurses, aides, and residents in a naming contest. To my sister and me, the monkey was unmistakably "Gertrude." But Mom insisted on her lengthier, more formal name. "Gertrude" became my mother's constant companion, and I quickly saw "more monkeys" move to the top of my to-do list.

"Gertrude" launched a four-month journey of unforeseen happiness, adding companionship, anticipation, and joy to each new day. Dozens of monkeys followed, and Mom hosted countless "sleep-overs" for her rapidly expanding group of friends. The new spark in Mom's eyes was never about me. It was the life force behind the monkeys themselves that formed the real gift. This new cast of characters carved out their own stories, each sending a taproot into Mom's most fanciful dreams and memories.

Mom's sock monkey journey was inexpressibly rich...a treasure trove of simple pleasures feeding her entire family. As she moved out of this life and into whatever follows, she cradled her friend, and I can only imagine she drew comfort from not passing alone.

GERTRUDE

Gertrude's heavily-lashed eyes and wide red lips complement her somewhat misshapen limbs and strangely fashionable attire. The "original" monkey, she's undeniably ahead of her time and out of step with convention, but she's captivating in her ingenuity. Gertrude developed a special fascination for genealogy in her later years and recently discovered that she grew up a mere four miles from her contemporary, Agatha. Photo courtesy of Rex-zane Rudee.

ABOUT THE AUTHOR

Shaped by a free-range childhood in the Pacific Northwest, the author's work radiates from a deep and playful inner space.

As one among billions being human on the planet, she pairs language with design for clarity, beauty, and impact. Centering love as its compass, One Being Human gathers artistry, whimsy, and humility for each project.

Sally Jo's tiny 450sf home kindled her passion for minimalism and helped stretch her into the song she's here to sing. She's animated by peace, poetry, gardening, cooking, and sock monkeys.